D0771095

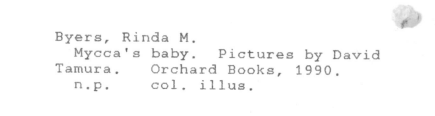

MYCCA'S BABY

BY RINDA M. BYERS

PICTURES BY DAVID TAMURA

ORCHARD BOOKS
A DIVISION OF FRANKLIN WATTS, INC./NEW YORK

Orchard Books
A division of Franklin Watts, Inc.
387 Park Avenue South, New York, New York 10016

The text of this book is set in 14 point Bembo.
The illustrations are oil paintings reproduced in full color.
Manufactured in the United States of America
Printed by General Offset Company, Inc.
Bound by Horowitz / Rae Book Manufacturers, Inc.
Book design by Sylvia Frezzolini

10 9 8 7 6 5 4 3 2 1

LIBRARY OF CONGRESS CATALOGING-IN-PUBLICATION DATA
Byers, Rinda M.   Mycca's baby / by Rinda M. Byers; pictures by David Tamura.
p.   cm.   Summary: When her Aunt Rose has a baby, Mycca wants to be a part of things and
have the baby be partly hers.
ISBN 0-531-05828-X. — ISBN 0-531-08428-0 (lib. bdg.)
[1. Aunts—Fiction.   2. Babies—Fiction.   3. Family life—Fiction.]   I. Tamura, David, ill.   II. Title.
PZ7.B98537My   1989   88-27320
[E]—dc19   CIP
                                                                 AC

FOR MY FAMILY R.B.
FOR MY MOTHER AND FATHER D.T.

n August, my Aunt Rose is going to have a baby. She is fat with that baby inside her. She is so fat, she can't get out of the car by herself.

"Mycca," she says, "help!"

I pull Rose's arms, but she is too heavy. Robert, her husband, has to help me. He pulls, and I pull, and we pull Rose out of the car.

"Uff!" says Rose. "I wish the baby was born. My feet hurt. And I look like a *pig*!"

I don't think Rose looks like a pig. I think she is beautiful. Robert thinks so too. He kisses her. Slowly. I wish a baby was coming to my house.

Robert plays a twelve-string guitar.
He makes up songs for Rose at night.
In the daytime, Robert works at the
feed store. He stops lifting the heavy
feed sacks so I can feel his muscles.

Robert is thin, but his muscles are
thick, hard ropes. He smells sweaty.
I give him a good slurp of my
ginger beer.

"Remember, Robert," I say,
"Grandma's fixing your lunch today."

Robert smiles at me.

"I won't forget," he says.

    Mama lets me eat lunch at Grandma's too. Robert eats slowly.
He eats three tuna fish sandwiches, a bowl of cherries, and six
chocolate cookies.

    "Robert, you better eat another sandwich," says Grandma.
"You are too thin. You work too hard."

    "O.K., Grandma," Robert answers. "You're the boss!" He eats
another sandwich.

    Grandma is canning cherries. Slip-slop, go her slippers. Slip-slop,
to the stove. Slip-slop, to the sink. Slip-slop, all over the kitchen.

Rose is folding clean sheets, stiff and crackly. Grandpa is reading the mail. Old Smokey, Grandma's cat, sits on the window sill with me.

"Rose, are you taking those vitamins I bought you?" Grandma asks.

"Yes," answers Rose. "Every single day!"

"Rose looks healthy to me," says Grandpa. "Don't fuss, Mother."

"I'll be glad when the baby's here," answers Grandma. "Then I won't worry."

"*I'll* be glad, too," Rose says. She winks at me. Robert eats three **more** cookies.

"The baby can sleep in our spare room while you're working, Rose," Grandma says. "The crib is all fixed up. And I bought thirty diapers on sale yesterday."

"Don't you have enough grandchildren, Mother?" Grandpa asks. "You have eight already!"

Grandma flips her apron at him.

"I don't care what *you* think," she says. "I just love babies. Besides, this one is special. This is Rose's first baby. Look, Rose, I have your old baby clothes here, washed and ironed. All ready for your own baby."

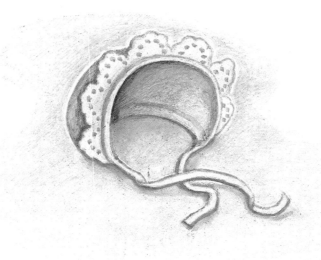

"They're still as good as new," says Rose softly. "Oh, thank you! Look, Robert!"

She touches the little clothes gently. I pick up a white baby cap. On it are lace and pink flowers. It is so tiny.

"Rose was the prettiest baby," says Grandma. "Remember, Father?"

"I remember," answers Grandpa. "She looked just like me!"

Everyone laughs, even Grandpa. And I sing softly into Old Smokey's ear, "A baby is coming, a baby is coming, a baby is coming soon!"

That afternoon, I walk home with Rose. She works hard even though she's fat. She takes care of the trailer where she and Robert live. She also takes care of Maudie next door.

Maudie is wrinkled, with gray hair and no teeth. She likes yellow and she walks with a walker. She forgets everything.

"Hi! Who are you?" she asks me.

"This is Mycca," Rose answers. "Remember? Mycca's been here before."

"Oh! That's nice!" says Maudie. She claps her hands. "And who are you?"

Rose sighs. "I'm Rose, remember?" she says. "I take care of you every day."

"I'm glad you came," says Maudie. She pats Rose's cheek. "I like to see a pretty face!"

"Sit down here, Maudie," Rose says. "See, here is your afghan. You can crochet and watch TV. Mycca and I will clean the kitchen."

The kitchen smells bad. Maudie has baked cookies, and the cookie pans are burned black. Rose and I have to throw all the cookies away. I scrub the cookie pans while Rose makes chicken potato soup for Maudie.

"Are you scared to have a baby?" I ask.

"A little," Rose answers. "But your mama and grandma are going to the hospital with me and Robert. I won't be very scared."

"Yeah," I say. "Grandma will tell the doctors what to do."

Rose laughs. "I think you're right," she says.

I want to ask Rose if I can help take care of the baby. I can't say the words. My throat's all stuck. What if Rose says no?

My brother, Ikie, used to be the baby in my house. He's three years old, and he's too big for me to hold. He hates being called Baby.

That night, I ask Mama, "Can't we have a new baby in our house?"

Mama shakes her head.

"Papa and I already have you and Ikie," she says. "The house is full. And a baby would be a lot of extra work."

"A baby could sleep in my room," I say. "I would take care of it. You would not have extra work."

Mama hugs me.

"I understand, Mycca," she says. "Babies are sweet. And you are a good helper. But you must wait until you have your own baby someday."

I don't like what Mama says. Someday is a long time. So I talk to Papa.

He is smoking his pipe and reading a comic book. He puts the comic book down, and I climb into his lap.

"What is it, Chicken?" he asks.

"Papa," I say, "we *need* a baby in our house."

Papa shakes his head too.

"We can't have a baby, Mycca," he says. "I barely earn enough money for you and Mama and Ikie. Besides, you'll get to share Rose's baby."

I know Papa is right about the money. I don't say anything more. But it isn't fair. Rose's baby will be her baby and Robert's baby. It won't be my baby.

Rose goes to the hospital early the next morning with Robert and Mama. Grandma and Grandpa go too. Papa stays home to take care of me and Ikie.

We eat toast and goopy eggs for breakfast. We eat cheese sandwiches for lunch. We eat macaroni and cheese for supper. We wait and wait and wait. And pretend to watch TV.

Finally, the phone rings. I answer it, and Mama is talking. She sounds sniffly.

"Did Rose have the baby?" I ask.

"No!" snaps Mama. "Get me Papa on the phone. Right now!"

I get Papa right now. He talks to Mama for a long time.

"Hi! Uh humm. Really? Yeah. Fine, fine. Yeah. O.K."

I stand on one foot. I stand on the other foot. I itch my elbow. My head hurts. I swing my arms around and around.

At last, Papa puts the phone down.

"Is Rose O.K.?" I ask.

"She's O.K.," Papa answers. "Mama says the baby is taking a long time and will be here later tonight. Now! Bedtime for you two. Hop! Hop!"

Ikie and I hop to bed fast. But I can't sleep. Will the baby be O.K.? Will it be a boy? Will it be a girl? What will it look like?

Ikie can't sleep either. He misses Mama. He peeks inside my bedroom and pitter-patters over to my bed with Monkey and his blanket.

"Mama," he says. "Mama."

"Mama'll be here soon, Ikie," I say. "You can sleep with me. Monkey can come too."

Ikie curls up close to me. I put my arms around him, and we go to sleep.

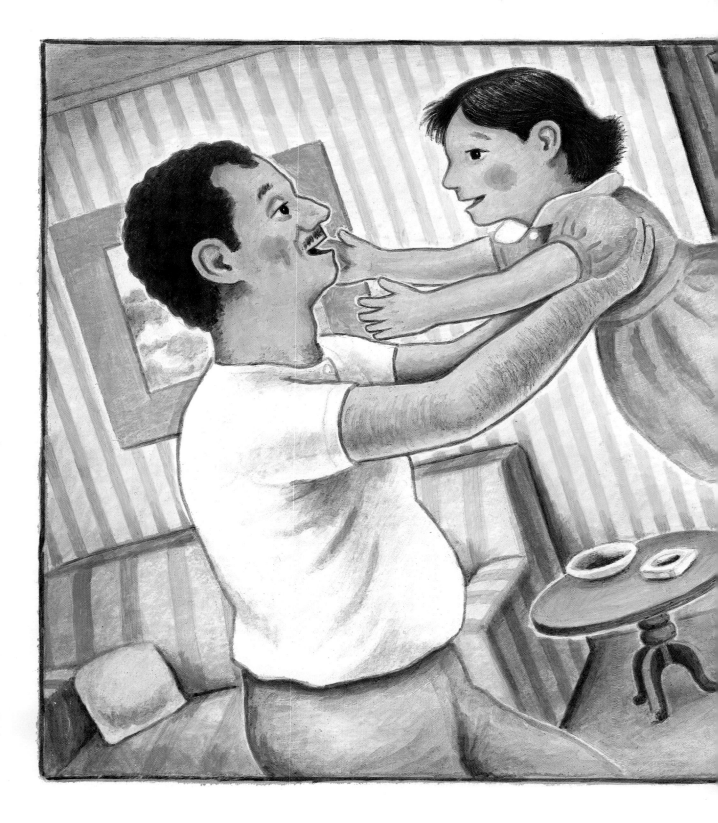

Ikie and I wake up when Mama comes home. It is morning. Mama's eyes are red. Papa hugs her tight and pats her back.

"I want you to go straight to bed," he says. "Right now."

Mama does not say one word. She goes to bed with her jeans and shirt and sandals on. Papa covers her up and shuts the bedroom door.

"What's wrong with Mama?" I ask.

"She's tired," Papa answers. "She was up all night. Mama's O.K., Mycca. Aunt Rose is O.K. too."

"Papa! The baby!" I say.

"The baby?" asks Papa. "What about the baby?" He's smiling. His blue eyes are twinkling stars at me.

I pull Papa's tee-shirt. Hard.

"Papa!" I say again. "The *baby*!!"

Papa starts laughing. He picks me up and swings me high.

"The baby," says Papa, "is a perfect little girl. Her name is Serenity."

The next day, Robert, Mama, Grandma, and Grandpa go to the hospital to pick up Rose and Serenity. I can't go.

"I'm sorry, Mycca," Mama says. "Rose is tired. She may need to lie down in the car. There isn't room for you."

Papa and Ikie are getting Mama's car fixed. So I stay alone at Grandma's house with Old Smokey. And I wait. I wait and I wait.

The house is quiet. It is sleeping. Old Smokey is sleeping too, on the window sill. I tiptoe through all the rooms.

Then, far away, I hear a car coming down the hill. I run outside. It is Robert's car. Rose is sitting beside Robert. She waves to me as he stops the car with a big swoosh.

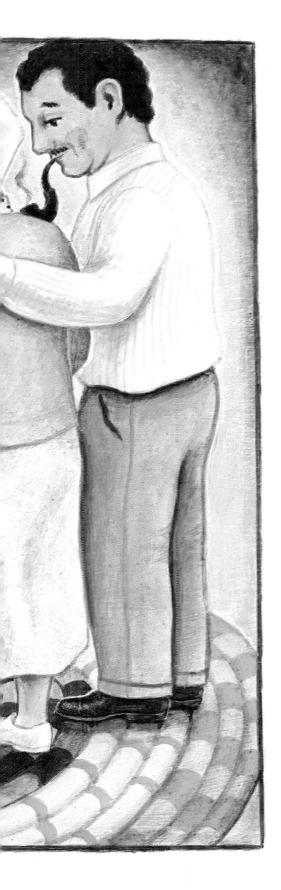

Suddenly, Grandma's house is full of noise. Everyone is talking very loudly all at once. And I get squished.

"Please, I want to see the baby," I say very politely. But no one listens.

"I still think Serenity looks just like me," says Grandpa.

"No, no, Father," says Grandma. "She has Rose's eyes and Robert's nose."

"She has my long fingers, too," says Robert. "She'll be a good guitar player."

"Here! Let me hold her, now," says Mama. "No, Grandma, you had your turn. This baby doesn't look like anyone in the family to me!"

I twist my neck, but all I see are blankets. My throat aches, and I want to cry. I can't say anything.

Rose is sitting in Grandpa's big chair. Her face is very white, but her eyes are full of secrets.

She says softly, "Robert, give me the baby. Mycca, sit down by me."

I sit down. Rose is smiling at me. Robert is smiling, too. Gently, Rose puts the baby in my arms.

"The baby has Robert's nose," says Rose. "She has my eyes. But she smiles just like Mycca!"

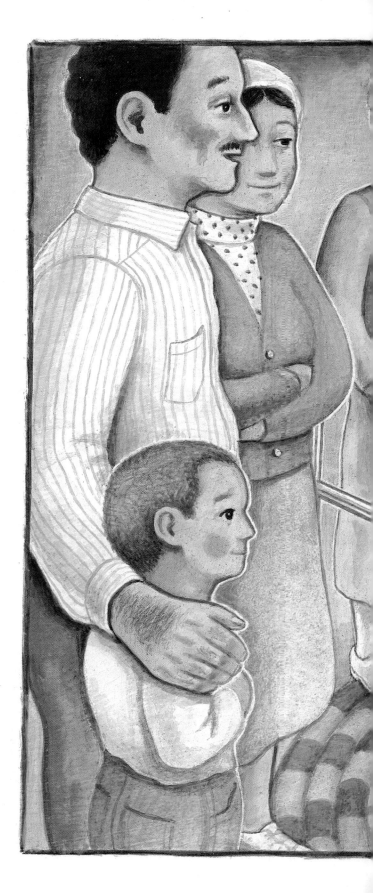

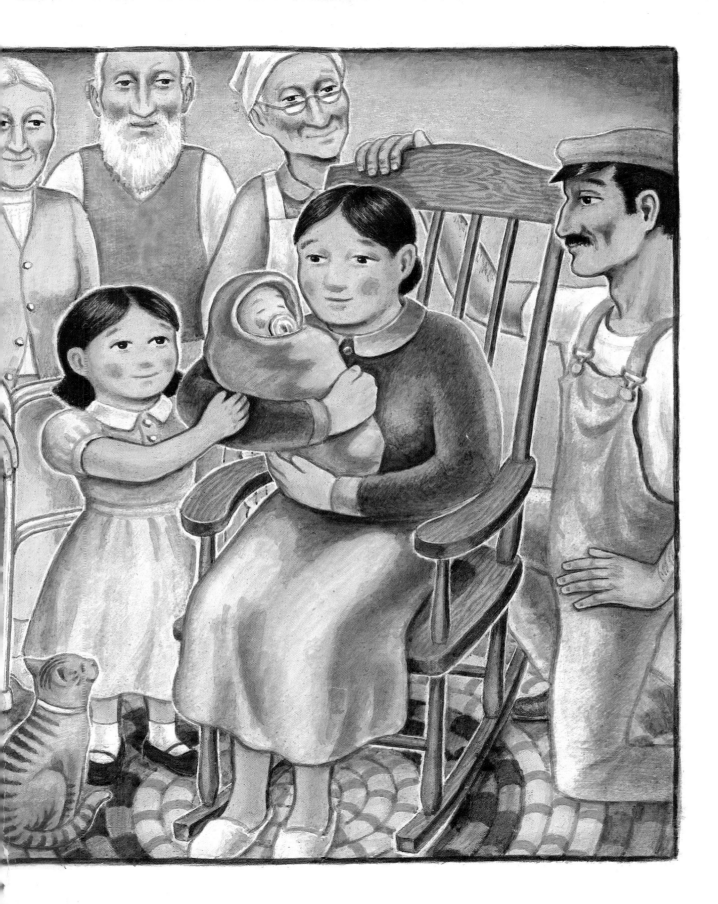

Serenity is heavy. And warm. Her eyes are open. Her hair is
black and straight. She is so pretty. Quick as a butterfly, she smiles.
   And I know.
   Serenity is Rose's baby. She is Robert's baby.
   She is my baby, too.